Making Tacos

Heather Hammonds
Photographs by Lindsay Edwards

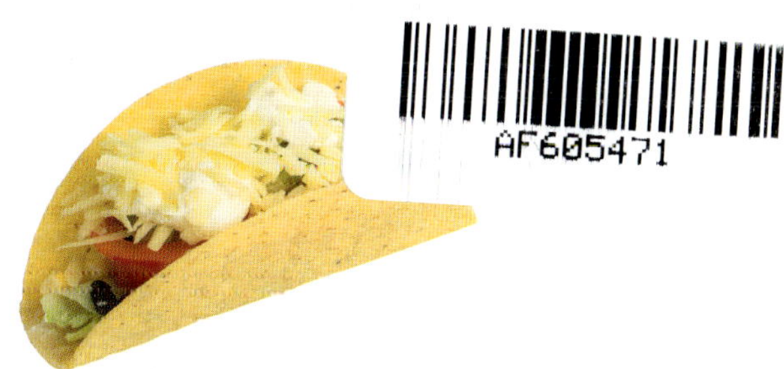

Contents

Goal 2
Foods 2
Kitchen Tools 4
Steps 6
Glossary 16

Goal

To make some tacos to eat for lunch or dinner

Foods

You will need:

- a can of black beans

- a can of corn

- two tomatoes

- a red capsicum

- a lettuce

- an avocado

- a tub of sour cream

- a block of cheese

- six large **taco shells.**

Kitchen Tools

You will need:

- a **strainer**

- seven bowls

- spoons and tongs

- a tea towel

- a chopping board and knife

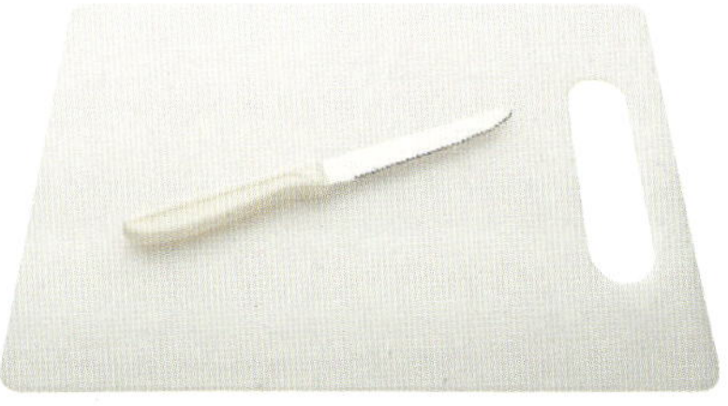

- a cheese **grater**

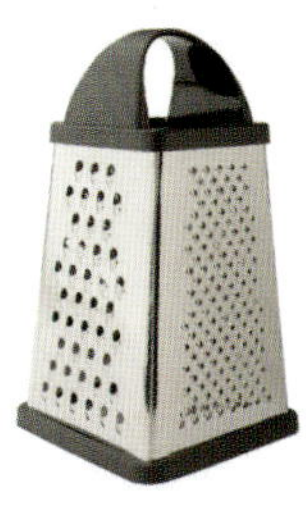

- an **oven**

- an oven tray

- oven gloves
- a big plate.

Steps

Wash your hands before you begin.

Getting All the Food Ready

1. Open the cans of black beans and corn. Ask an adult to help you.

2. Put the beans and corn into the strainer together. Rinse them with clean water over the sink.

3. Now, put the beans and corn into a bowl and mix them together with a spoon.

4. Wash the tomatoes and capsicum. Use the tea towel to dry them.

5. Pull the lettuce apart and wash each of the leaves. Dry them with the tea towel, too.

6. Ask an adult to cut the avocado in half and take the stone out of it.

7. Use your fingers to gently peel the skin off the avocado.

8. Cut the tomatoes, avocado and capsicum into lots of little pieces. Ask an adult to help you do this.

9. Put the pieces of tomato, avocado and capsicum into three bowls.

10. Tear the lettuce leaves into lots of little pieces and put them into a bowl, too.

11. Open the tub of sour cream and use a spoon to put it into a bowl.

12. Grate some cheese and put it into a bowl, too.

Filling the Taco Shells

1. Ask an adult to turn the oven on.
2. Lay the six taco shells in a row, on an oven tray.

3. Now, ask an adult to put the taco shells into the oven for 5 minutes, to warm them up.

It is important not to let the taco shells get too hot!

4. Ask an adult to put the warm taco shells onto the big plate.

5. Pick up a taco shell and use the tongs to carefully put some lettuce into the bottom of it.

6. Use a small spoon to put some of the mixed beans and corn on top of the lettuce.

7. Now, put some tomato on top of the beans and corn.

8. Put some capsicum and avocado on top of the tomato.

9. Next, put one spoonful of sour cream on top of all the foods inside the taco.

10. Sprinkle some of the grated cheese on top of the sour cream.

11. Fill the rest of the taco shells in the same way and put them all on the big plate.

The tacos are now ready to eat!

Glossary

grater (*noun*) a kitchen tool that cuts food like cheese into lots of small bits

oven (*noun*) a kitchen tool used to cook or heat up food

strainer (*noun*) a bowl with lots of little holes in it for washing food

taco shells (*noun*) hard, thin shells, often made from corn